CW0670867

# THE
# DREAM QUILT

# THE
# DREAM QUILT

Adèle Geras

*Illustrated by Valerie Greeley*

For Lucy
Happy Birthday
+ love from
Adèle
x

LONG BARN BOOKS

PUBLISHED BY
LONG BARN BOOKS

Printed and bound by
JFDi Print Services Ltd.

ISBN: 978-1-902421-60-5

*For Nathan Joshua Geras Jones*
A.G.


*For Edie and George Corrigan*
V.G.

I threaded silk through a silver needle
to make a cover for your bed.
Rest your head
Close your eyes.
I'll stitch you dreams and lullabies.

Here is a house.

Everyone's sleeping,
except a child
who wants to know
what everybody's dream might be;
and when they close their eyes at night,
what do they see?

> Follow the stitches
> As they are made.
> Blue and silver.
> Light and shade.

Here is a doll
dreaming of walking
down the path to another house.
She dreams of a party
and drinking tea
with all the friends
she has gone to see.

The narrow path that twists and bends
dreams of bringing you home
when your journey ends.

Follow the silks
as they unwind.
What do you find
As the silks unwind?

Here is a bear
who is brown and small
and wants to speak
in a small brown voice
so you can hear
the tales he tells
of big black bears
in caves of stone.
He whispers gently
in your ear:
"Look, here I am.
You are not alone."

The dark cave dreams of sheltering
Mother and Father and Baby Bear,
keeping them dry, keeping them warm
safe and cosy out of the storm.

Follow the stitches
as they are made.
Grey and gold.
Light and shade.

Here is a rocking horse
standing still,
imagining fields
he can gallop through
when the moon is full
and the air is blue
and a green wind blows
from over the hill.

What the moon would love
is a mile of space
and no thin clouds to cover her face.

As the silks unwind,
What do you find?
Follow the silks.
What do you find?

Here is a kitten
with four white paws
on a rainbow day
in the meadow green.
She dreams of creeping
through the grass
catching the butterflies
she has seen
who tickle her white nose
as they pass.

Out in the meadow
a rainbow curves
and as it fades
it longs to stay
fixed in its colours
for one whole day.

Follow the stitches.
Light and shade.
Green and purple
as they are made.

Here is a ball,
rolling and rolling,
waiting to fly
from hand to hand,
waiting for beaches,
waiting for summer,
waiting for castles
made of sand.

The shell says, "Listen, listen to me.
Can you hear the sea, the sea, the sea?

What do you find?
What do you find?
Follow the silks
as they unwind.

Here is a ship
with masts and spars
reaching up
to the silent stars.
This is a ship
that longs for an ocean
and longs to hear
the songs that are sung
under the water
in emerald caves
by the King of the Sea
and his mermaid daughter.

Up in the sky the small stars glow
wanting the ship to follow their light
into the morning, out of the night.

Follow the stitches
as they are made.
Blue and white.
Light and shade.

Here is a train
that wants to run
clackety clack
along the track
all the way
to far away
and all the way
back.

The mountain waits for a cloak of snow
when the winter comes and the blizzards blow.

Follow the silks
as the silks unwind.
What do you find?
What do you find?

Here is a tiger
dreaming of jungles,
silent and shadowy
full of prey.
He dreams of roaring
snarling, clawing
and an afternoon sleep
in the heat of the day.

A forest needs to be deep and wide
and dark to hide what it has to hide.

Orange and black.
Light and shade.
Follow the stitches
as they are made.

Here is a rabbit
with pink glass eyes
who dreams of carrots
in long straight rows.
He dreams of an open garden gate
and a place where frilly lettuce grows.

The garden waits for a summer day
and fuzzy bees to buzz and play.

As the silks unwind
what do you find?
Follow the silks.
What do you find?

Here is a fish
in a bowl of glass
dreaming of water flowing fast.
Dreaming of sliding and hiding away
by the riverbank
in the reeds and grass.

As the river runs
it longs to reach
the wide grey sea,
the pebbly beach.

Green and gold
as they are made.
Follow the stitches.
Light and shade.

Here is a bird
who wants to fly
out of the cage
with the golden bars,
out of the window
into the sky
where every tree
calls out and sings:
"Try it! Open them!
Spread your wings."

This is the wish of every tree:
for birds to settle and fold their wings.
and flutter and cry and coo and call
till the autumn comes and the red leaves fall.

What do you find?
What do you find?
Follow the silks
as the silks unwind.

Here is a pillow
soft and white
filled with every dream we know,
and also filled with songs that tell
where dreams come from,
where they go.

The silver needle moves in and out
pricking the fabric, pulling the thread.
I've stitched a cover to keep you warm
dreaming dreams in your quiet bed.

You followed the silks
as the silks unwound.
Rest your head,
close your eyes.
Remember all the dreams you found.

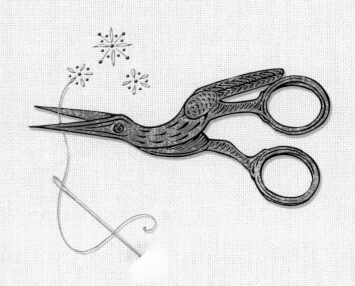